For Mimi, with my love

GUMDROP
AND THE PIRATES

Story and pictures by Val Biro

HODDER AND STOUGHTON
LONDON SYDNEY AUCKLAND TORONTO

MR JOSIAH OLDCASTLE was sitting in Gumdrop, his trusty old vintage car. His grandson Dan sat in the back with Horace the dog next to him. They were at the seaside having their picnic, so they should have been enjoying themselves.

Unfortunately it was raining – positively pouring down. On their holiday too, in the middle of July. So they were thoroughly fed up and miserable.

'Never mind,' said Mr Oldcastle, trying to cheer things up. 'Why don't you imagine that it is sunny and that Gumdrop's brass isn't going green with all this rain?' He knew that Dan was good at imagining things, so he left it to the boy and helped himself to a sandwich.

So Dan began to imagine that the sun was shining brightly – just as brightly as in the book he was reading. It was about a pirate called Blackendagger and Dan was just getting to the exciting bit. So he didn't notice that Horace had pinched his sausage-roll, but he *did* hear the dog's happy bark. Dan looked up, and to his utter amazement he saw that…

…the sun had come out and Horace was scampering around in the dry grass! Dan thought that he was just imagining all this, but there was Mr Oldcastle himself, strolling around in the warm sunshine.

So Dan leapt out of Gumdrop and ran down to the shore. When he got there he nearly jumped out of his skin.

'Look at *that*!' he yelled and pointed.

A huge ship had suddenly appeared, rounding the bay: a pirate ship with a black flag at the mast. Just like the one in Dan's book, except that this one was heading straight towards them!

'Pirates, my goodness!' cried Mr Oldcastle.
'They can be dangerous and those men on board
look particularly nasty. Come on Dan, come
Horace, we'd better get back into Gumdrop quickly!'

By then the ship had anchored. The pirates were pouring
ashore and they were led by Captain Blackendagger himself!
They were certainly a nasty-looking bunch, but when they
saw Gumdrop they ran in terror and hid behind some rocks.
They must have thought that Gumdrop was a blue sea-monster.

Captain Blackendagger would have run away too, but he tripped over his sword and went sprawling. He staggered to his feet, but the black patch he wore over one eye slipped and now he could see Gumdrop with both eyes.

'This ain't a monster,' he yelled, 'it's a horseless carriage, by thunder!'

The other pirates were relieved to hear that this strange carriage was horseless, so they stopped hiding and advanced menacingly.

'Stand clear!' warned Mr Oldcastle. 'Let me tell you that
my carriage has no less than twelve horses under the bonnet!'
He revved up the engine to prove how fierce they were, and
Gumdrop obligingly produced a fearful kicking noise.

The pirates were frightened of horses, not having seen any
during all their twelve years at sea. So they promptly ran
off again.

Mr Oldcastle got out and made an offer. 'I shall keep my horses under control provided you keep your thieving fingers off my car.'

The pirates calmed down and promised to behave themselves. In fact they agreed to be friends, and Mr Oldcastle shook hands with Captain Blackendagger.

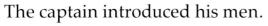

The captain introduced his men.
'The tall one is Titch, the short one's Lofty, the fat one's Skinny, the bald one's Fuzz and Pegleg is the peg-legged one.'

Then Captain Blackendagger took off his pirate's hat and gave it to Dan, as proof of his friendship.

'But we have a job to do,' he said. 'We've come to collect our buried treasure, but my deadly enemy Captain Rattlesabre is on his way too and he might get it first. So we must hurry!'

'Let's take them in Gumdrop,' cried Dan, adjusting his big hat. 'After all I am a pirate now and they're our partners!'

Mr Oldcastle agreed and
folded down Gumdrop's hood.
The pirates piled in, with two
on the running-boards and Lofty on
the luggage grid. 'Hold tight!' cried
Mr Oldcastle and they were off.

   They drove up the coast until they reached another bay.
Titch was the tallest, so he acted as lookout with a telescope.
Suddenly he cried, 'Deck ahoy! Ship on the port bow!'

It was another huge pirate ship riding at anchor. 'Shiver my timbers,' roared Captain Blackendagger, 'it's Rattlesabre's ship! The villain's ahead of us. Come on lads, after them!' And they all leapt out of Gumdrop to find the enemy.

There was no one to be seen. 'They must have gone to look for my treasure,' wailed Captain Blackendagger, 'but I don't know which way they went!' He was a very inefficient pirate; he had left his map behind and couldn't remember the way. So he burst into tears.

'What's this?' asked Dan, picking up a feather.
'A parrot's feather!' cried Fuzz.
'There ain't no parrots here,' said Pegleg.
'But Rattlesabre's got one!' declared Skinny.

'That's it!' exclaimed Mr Oldcastle, and called
Horace. 'My dog will find the way!' Horace
smelled the feather and snarled, because he
hated parrots. 'Search, boy, search!' said
Mr Oldcastle and Horace was off like a shot.

'After him!' they cried, and leapt back into Gumdrop. They could hardly keep up with Horace who was hot on the scent, barking like a foxhound. The pirates waved their swords and yelled, 'Tally-ho! Parrot's away! View-halloo!' Mr Oldcastle hooted the horn for good measure and Gumdrop bucked along like a hunting-horse.

Horace knew exactly where that parrot had gone and he streaked
ahead, quick as lightning. Suddenly he stopped with his nose
in the air, quivering all over. Because straight in front of
him the bushes parted, and out came…

...the parrot! It was sitting on Captain Rattlesabre's shoulder. The captain was surrounded by his fierce pirates, and two of the fiercest were carrying a huge treasure chest.

'There's my treasure,' yelled Captain Blackendagger, 'stand and deliver!' He leapt out of Gumdrop but in his excitement he tripped again and knocked his pirates into a heap. Horace took no notice but charged – straight at the parrot.

The parrot looked scared and leapt off the captain's shoulder. 'Get away! Bad boy! Get away!' she squawked as Horace chased her. She was too fat to fly, but she ran fast enough. She managed to reach a tree just in time, and she hopped into a hole where the dog couldn't get at her. So Horace sat in front of the hole and waited, with his tongue hanging out.

Captain Rattlesabre and his men were frightened. To be attacked by pirates in a car was bad enough, but what really terrified them was Horace: they hadn't seen a dog during all their twelve years at sea, and this one looked vicious. The men were about to run away, when Captain Rattlesabre burst into tears.

'My parrot,' he wailed, 'I want my parrot! I've had her for forty years and I want her back!' But he dared not attack the dog, in case Horace bit him.

'My treasure,' roared Captain Blackendagger, 'it's mine and I want it back!' But he dared not attack his enemy, because Captain Rattlesabre was bigger than him.

'My goodness,' exclaimed Mr Oldcastle,
'we can't have this! I tell you what,
Captain Rattlesabre. You give half
the treasure to Blackendagger here,
I'll call off my dog and you can
have your parrot.'

Captain Rattlesabre agreed, because he loved his parrot
and she was worth half the treasure. Captain Blackendagger
agreed, because half the treasure was better than none.
Even Horace agreed to leave the parrot, though he would
have liked it for his lunch.

So all was well. The captains
promised to be friends and shook
hands, and Rattlesabre and his
pirates returned to their ship
with half the treasure – and the parrot.

Captain Blackendagger was very grateful, and patted Gumdrop for helping to find the treasure. He offered a large reward, but Mr Oldcastle would accept only one coin from the heap of Spanish doubloons in the chest.

'And perhaps that bottle of brandy,' he suggested.

So they shook hands all around, Titch and Fuzz picked up the chest with half the treasure, and Captain Blackendagger and his pirates marched back to their ship, singing a merry shanty.

'Well,' said Mr Oldcastle, 'we deserve a drink after all that!' He poured some of the brandy and gave a little to Dan as well.

It was then that Dan's imagination stopped working, for he just couldn't imagine what brandy tasted like…

…It tasted just like orange juice, nice and cold.
They were back at the seaside, finishing their picnic.
Dan saw that the rain had really stopped this time and
the sun was shining brightly.

'There you are, my boy,' said Mr Oldcastle, 'I told
you to use your imagination, and in this case it must
have worked overtime!'

Which it certainly had, you must admit.

Or was it just imagination? Because when Mr Oldcastle
tidied up the picnic things, there, right on the back seat
of Gumdrop, he found a brandy bottle,
a Spanish doubloon
and a pirate's hat.

And Horace held a parrot's feather in his mouth.

British Library Cataloguing in Publication Data

Biro, Val
Gumdrop and the pirates.
I. Title
823'.914 [J]

ISBN 0-340-50123-5

First published 1989

Published by Hodder and Stoughton Children's Books,
a division of Hodder and Stoughton Ltd,
Mill Road, Dunton Green, Sevenoaks, Kent TN13 2YA

Printed in Great Britain by Cambus Litho, East Kilbride